SKY BIKERS

BY TONY NORMAN

ILLUSTRATED BY PAUL SAVAGE
COVER ILLUSTRATED BY MARCUS SMITH

jN
E

Librarian Reviewer
Marci Peschke
Librarian, Dallas Independent School District
MA Education Reading Specialist, Stephen F. Austin State University
Learning Resources Endorsement, Texas Women's University

Reading Consultant
Mary Evenson
Middle School Teacher, Edina Public Schools, MN
MA in Education, University of Minnesota

 **STONE ARCH BOOKS**
Minneapolis   San Diego

First published in the United States in 2008
by Stone Arch Books
151 Good Counsel Drive, P.O. Box 669
Mankato, Minnesota 56002
www.stonearchbooks.com

Originally published in Great Britain in 2006
by Badger Publishing Ltd.

Library of Congress Cataloging-in-Publication Data
Norman, Tony.
    Sky Bikers / by Tony Norman; illustrated by Paul Savage.
    p. cm. — (Keystone Books)
    Summary: After hitting his head while riding a rusty old bicycle,
Tyler meets a very unusual girl who takes him on an impossible adventure
at the seashore.
    ISBN-13: 978-1-59889-851-4 (library binding)
    ISBN-10: 1-59889-851-5 (library binding)
    ISBN-13: 978-1-59889-903-0 (paperback)
    ISBN-10: 1-59889-903-1 (paperback)
    [1. Bicycles and bicycling—Fiction. 2. Seashore—Fiction.
3. Science fiction.] I. Savage, Paul, 1971– ill. II. Title.
PZ7.N7862Sky 2008
[Fic]—dc22   2007003019

1 2 3 4 5 6 12 11 10 09 08 07

TABLE OF CONTENTS

CHAPTER 1

TIME OUT

The summer sun beat down on the tall apartment building in the big city. It was already eleven, but Tyler was still in bed. He was bored out of his mind.

He didn't want to watch TV.

He didn't want to play video games.

He was sick and tired of all that stuff. Basketball. That's what he needed. A game of basketball.

Great idea! Tyler jumped out of bed and picked up two socks from the floor.

He rolled them into a ball. Then he threw the socks, and they flew across the room. He ran to pick them up.

"Tyler Stone is winning the game for the Panthers," Tyler yelled. "He's in the zone now. He shoots!"

Tyler tossed the socks into the wall above his bed.

They bounced back through the air.

"The ball hits the rim, but Tyler Stone rebounds and scores with an amazing jump!" Tyler yelled.

Tyler jumped up and grabbed the socks, before falling down on his bed.

The socks hit his schoolbooks, hard.
They fell to the floor with a crash.

The door flew open. Tyler's dad
stood there, looking angry.

Tyler knew his game was about to
get a time out!

CHAPTER 2

DAD'S IDEA

"Stop making so much noise," his dad snapped. "Why don't you go out and enjoy the sun?"

"There's nothing to do outside," said Tyler, in a sulky voice. "All my friends are on vacation. How come we're still stuck here in the city?"

Tyler's dad looked upset. He didn't have a job, so he couldn't pay for a vacation.

Tyler felt bad. "Sorry," he said.

"It's okay," said his dad. "I wish we could get away too. But I heard there's a summer camp down at the skate park. How does that sound?"

"Cool," said Tyler, with a grin.

"Okay, get your board," said Dad. He smiled. "I'll walk down there with you. Let's go!"

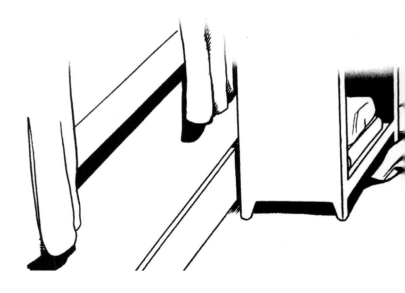

It took Tyler a while to find his skateboard.

Finally he found it. It was buried deep under his bed.

There were cobwebs all over it because he never used it.

The truth was, Tyler had lied to make his dad happy.

The skate park was probably the last place in the whole wide world that Tyler wanted to go.

Especially during his summer break.

CHAPTER 3

SKATE PARK CRASH

At the skate park, Tyler was given a helmet, knee pads, and elbow pads to wear.

He sat on a bench to put them on.

The skate park was full of kids doing tricks on the ramps.

Loud music was playing.

All the other kids looked really happy.

Everyone else seemed to be having a lot of fun.

What am I doing here? thought Tyler.

He didn't know any of the other kids. They all looked good on their skateboards.

They all knew cool moves and difficult tricks.

Tyler knew he would look stupid on the ramps. So he sat on the bench all by himself.

He looked around the skate park.
Then he smiled.

A rusty old bike lay by the fence.
Tyler loved bikes.

He quickly put his
helmet on. Then he
ran over, jumped on
the rusty old
bike, and
started doing
wheelies.

Soon the other kids were watching him.

Tyler decided to put on a show
for them.

He did a couple of wheelies, but that
didn't seem very interesting.

He was worried the other kids would
get bored watching his show.

Then he rode the bike up one of the
skate park ramps.

He tried to spin and come back down, but he was going too fast and he fell.

Tyler's head hit the hard ramp and the rusty bike crashed to the ground.

CHAPTER 4

LIENA

Tyler opened his eyes.

A girl with shiny purple skin was looking down at him.

Tyler shut his eyes, and then opened them again.

The girl was still there.

"Are you okay?" she asked.

Her voice sounded like the notes of a music box.

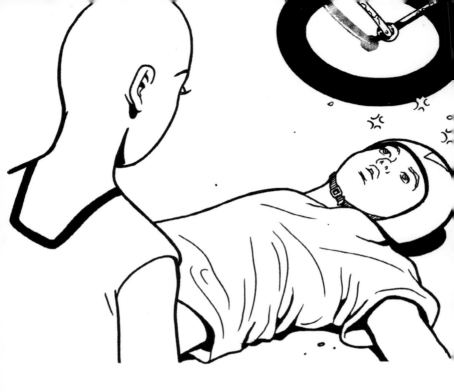

Her eyes were yellow and she had no hair on her head, but she was still pretty.

"Are you an alien?" asked Tyler.

"No," said the girl, smiling.

"I hit my head and this is just a crazy dream, right?" Tyler said.

"No, you can believe in me," said the girl. "My name is Liena. Your name is Tyler. I can read your mind."

"Yeah, right," said Tyler.

"All your friends are away on vacation, so you are not happy," said Liena. "But you can see the beach today. I will take you."

"How?" asked Tyler.

"Ride that bike as fast as you can," Liena said.

"Then what, crash again?" Tyler shook his head.

"No, trust me," said Liena. "And if you are dreaming, what do you have to lose?"

"This is so weird," Tyler said. He got on the bike. "Okay."

Tyler started to pedal as fast as he could. The bike began to shake, as if it were coming alive. Then, in a split second, the rusty old bike turned to silver.

 **CHAPTER 5**

SKY BIKE RIDER

Tyler saw a rush of bright colors speed past his eyes. Then he was riding his bright silver bike through the sky. Liena was flying beside him.

"Tyler," Liena shouted, "you are now a Sky Bike Rider!"

Tyler's mind was in a spin. "I don't know if this is real or a dream," he said. "But who cares?"

"Ready to race?" asked Liena.

"Go for it!" yelled Tyler.

And with that they raced off across the clear blue summer sky. They flew up toward the sun, then raced down through soft white clouds like cotton balls. Tyler felt like he was on the best theme park ride ever.

Liena smiled at him and pointed down. Tyler saw a bright yellow beach far below them.

Liena dove, and he followed.

Soon they were standing on the hot yellow sand.

Liena ran and dove into the waves.
Tyler swam in the sea too.

As they walked back up the beach,
Liena clicked her fingers and Tyler's
wet clothes dried like magic.

"Are you hungry?" Liena asked.

"I'd like some fries, ice cream, and cotton candy, please," said Tyler.

Liena snapped her fingers and Tyler found all the food in his hands.

After lunch they went on every
ride at a fair at the end of the beach.
Nobody else seemed to see Liena. Only
Tyler could.

Soon the sun started to slip from
the sky. "We should go back now,"
said Liena.

Tyler didn't want to leave, but the race back through the sky made him feel good again. Liena told him to slow down when they saw the skate park. But Tyler wanted to land in style, and he came in too fast.

The second the old bike hit the ground, it turned to rust again and Tyler fell to the ground.

CHAPTER 6

SEE YOU SOON

That night, Tyler lay in bed trying to make sense of it all.

When he woke up at the skate park, the other kids said he had hit his head when he fell off the old bike.

When Tyler asked them about a purple girl with yellow eyes, they all said he was acting crazy.

"Maybe they were right," Tyler thought.

"But then, why did my shoes have sand in them when I got home tonight?" he wondered aloud.

His head was sore and he felt sleepy. He didn't want to think any more. He turned off the light. He was almost asleep when his phone beeped. Tyler read the text message by the phone's soft green light.

Tyler tried to save the text, but he was so tired, he deleted it instead.

cu soon
sky bike rider!
liena x

He put the phone down in the dark.

Had Liena really sent him a message?

Tyler didn't know.

But he fell asleep with Liena's message in his mind.

"See you soon, Sky Bike Rider!" Maybe the text would come true . . . just maybe.

ABOUT THE AUTHOR

Tony Norman is a children's writer and poet from the South Coast of England. He once played in a group in a school talent show. Tony still sings and plays guitar. Loyal fans include the frogs, toads, and fish in his garden pond!

ABOUT THE ILLUSTRATOR

Paul Savage works in a design studio, drawing pictures for advertising. He says illustrating books is "the best job." He's always been interested in illustrating books, and he loves reading. Paul also enjoys playing sports and running.

He lives in England with his wife and their daughter, Amelia.

GLOSSARY

alien (AY-lee-uhn)—someone from a different country or planet

apartment building (uh-PART-muhnt BIL-ding)—a large building made up of several smaller homes, which are called apartments

cobwebs (KOB-webz)—a net of sticky threads made by a spider to catch insects

deleted (di-LEE-tid)—erased words from a computer screen or cell phone message

dove (DOHV)—plunged, or dropped down quickly

sulky (SUHL-kee)—crabby or angry

text (TEKST)—written words or message; words on paper or a computer screen

vacation (vay-KAY-shuhn)—a trip away from home

DISCUSSION QUESTIONS

1. Tyler crashes his bike when he's trying to do tricks to impress the other kids at the skate park. Have you ever done something dangerous to impress others, or seen someone else do something dangerous? What did you or the other person do? What was the result? How could things have been different?

2. Have you ever heard other strange stories about a person who passed out and had a strange dream or experience, like Tyler did in this book? Talk about other stories you've heard like this one.

3. Why does Tyler agree to go to the skate park, even though he doesn't want to? What would you have done?

WRITING PROMPTS

1. It's hard to believe, but sometimes summer break can be boring! What are your favorite things to do on the weekend or when you're on summer break? Make a list.

2. At the end of this book, Tyler isn't sure whether he'll ever see Liena again. Write a short story about their next meeting. What do they do? Where do they go? Don't forget to describe the details of the places they go and the things they do.

3. If you move the letters around in Liena's name you can make the word "alien." Is that a clue to where the girl comes from? What do you think Liena's home is like? Describe a visit to Liena's.

MORE BOOKS

Nervous

Elite is the best band in school. The Dream Stars Talent Show is the perfect chance for Jools and Cass to prove their new band is just as good, or even better.

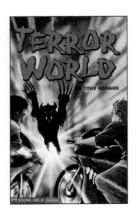

Terror World

Jimmy and Seb love playing the arcade games at Terror World. When the owner offers them a free trial on the newest, coolest video game, they enter into a real "Terror World."

BY TONY NORMAN

The Race of a Lifetime

Jamie's chances of winning the school bike race look good after he buys a new bike. Unfortunately, he runs into trouble before the race even begins.

INTERNET SITES

Do you want to know more about subjects related to this book? Or are you interested in learning about other topics? Then check out FactHound, a fun, easy way to find Internet sites.

Our investigative staff has already sniffed out great sites for you!

Here's how to use FactHound:

1. Visit *www.facthound.com*

2. Select your grade level.

3. To learn more about subjects related to this book, type in the book's ISBN number: **1598898515**.

4. Click the **Fetch It** button.

FactHound will fetch the best Internet sites for you!